A River Lost

by L. E. Bragg
illustrated by V. "Smoker" Marchand

hancock

house

Dedication

This book is dedicated to the People of the Town of Inchelium, especially my son, Patrick, and the Marchand children.

Acknowledgments

Special Thanks to: Marguerite Ensminger, for the translations; my mom, Polly Bragg, for editing; my family; and, to my friends at Miller, Nash for your support!

ISBN 0-88839-383-0
Copyright © Lynn Bragg

Cataloging in Publication Data
Bragg, Lynn E., 1956-
    A river lost
    ISBN 0-88839-383-0
    1. British Columbia–Arrow Lakes Region-Juvenile literature. 2. Grand Coulee Dam (Wash.)–Environmental aspects–Juvenile literature. 3. Salmon fisheries–British Columbia–Arrow Lakes Region-Juvenile literature. 4. Salmon–Effect of dams on–Juvenile literature. I. Marchand, Virgil. II. Title.
E78.B9B76 1995   j971.1'6200497   C95-911015-1

Copy edit: Nancy Kerr
Production: Lorna Brown

Published simultaneously in Canada and the United States by

HANCOCK HOUSE PUBLISHERS LTD.
19313 Zero Avenue, Surrey, B.C. V4P 1M7
(604) 538-1114   Fax (604) 538-2262

HANCOCK HOUSE PUBLISHERS
1431 Harrison Avenue, Blaine, WA 98230-5005
(604) 538-1114   Fax (604) 538-2262

Prologue

A River Lost is the story of an ancient culture forever changed by modern technology. It is the story of my son's tribe, The Arrow Lakes Tribe, now part of the Colville Confederated Tribes. For thousands of years this tribe's way of life revolved around the Columbia River, and fishing for salmon at the river's falls. All of this was taken away from them during "The New Deal" when Grand Coulee Dam was built.

The dam had no fish ladders, hence the salmon could never return to this once fertile fishing site. The dam also wiped out the entire town of Inchelium with very little advance notice to the town's residents. Many elders of the Tribe did not believe this could really happen, and, therefore many of them did not move their homes out of the path of the oncoming water until the last possible moment. The Colville Tribal Members finally received payment, promised to them when the dam was built in the 1930s, on April 7, 1995!

Toopa refused to believe what was happening. I stood with my great-grandmother, Toopa, on the porch of the home she had lived in all of her adult life. We watched smoke rising from the fires below. As night fell, the sky took on a yellow glow and flickering orange flames lit up the horizon.

Toopa's little clapboard cabin was nestled against the hillside, on the banks of the River. Behind the rustic structure, brown hills, dotted with sweet-smelling pine trees, rolled upward toward dense forests. Beyond the rickety front porch lay the mighty River that was the lifeline to our people.

The acrid, smoky smell filled the night air. Houses that
had not been moved were being burned to make way for
a man-made lake. The Indian Agent had told the people
of my tribe that they must move their entire village, or it
would be destroyed by the rising waters behind the
Grand Dam the government had built.

This massive concrete dam would change our way of life
forever, taking from us our sacred River and precious
salmon, or In-Tee-Tee-**Huh**. For thousands of years my
people had taken their food, traveled, and met at the
River and the River's Falls.

The rocks below the Falls had been hollowed out by the constant pummeling of the cascading River. These rocks, when full of water, looked like cooking kettles. Early fur traders called my people, *"Les Chaudieres,"* or *"Kettle Indians."*

9

Each summer families from our tribe traveled up the River to the Falls in search of food. The summer encampments brought families from tribes near and far to fish the River, trade, and visit friends and relatives. The Falls had been an important meeting place for generations. In the old days, when the salmon were running, hundreds of tepees and lodges had lined the banks of the Great River.

Coastal Indians crossed the Cascade Mountains, and
brought with them beautiful shells to trade. Plains Indians
came across the Rocky Mountains, bringing buffalo hides
and dried meat to trade for salmon. In turn, families from
my tribe had sometimes journeyed east into the plains to
hunt the buffalo.

Toopa folded her arms across her chest defiantly, *"How can man change the rushing waters of the River into the still waters of a lake?"* she scoffed. Like many of our elders, Toopa could not accept what was happening. It did not seem possible that man's actions could do this, turn our River and our land into a great lake! It was very difficult to convince great-grandmother that she must move.

It was time now for Toopa to leave her home. The Grand Dam was finished. Soon the waters of the new lake would begin rising behind the Dam. Toopa stayed in the house, refusing to watch as we harvested her beloved garden. Everything we wished to save had to be moved to higher ground. Homes, animals, gardens, and our church were moved. Even burial sites had to be dug up and moved uphill.

Only when great-grandmother could see the water rising, did she agree to leave her home. We had very little time before the rising tide of water would flood the place where our village had stood. As I helped Toopa pack her possessions she seemed sad and was silent. Then, in a dust-covered box, she found an old picture of herself as a small girl at her family's summer camp near the Falls.

Her dark eyes grew bright with memories of her childhood as she began to speak. *"You know, Sinee mat,"* Toopa paused, and leaned against a stack of boxes, *"every summer my family camped at the Falls. When the salmon swam upstream to spawn, the water became so thick and matted with their red bodies that it looked as if you could walk across the River on the backs of the In-Tee-Tee-***Huh***.*

"It was my job to help my mother prepare for our summer home at the Falls. Mother and I gathered cooking utensils, food, woven mats, and skins for bedding. Father packed his spears, gaff hooks, and baskets used for fishing the Falls. My baby brother was laced tightly into his cradleboard for the journey up the River.

"Our family traveled up the River as far as possible in a pine-bark canoe that father had stretched over a cedar frame. The River was calm at first, but soon became turbulent. When the water became too rough, we continued our trip to the Falls on foot. Our home for the summer was a deerskin tepee at the base of the Falls.

17

"*Once at the camp, my Sinee mat,*" Toopa continued, her eyes sparkling with life, "*every person had chores to do. Even the littlest child helped by gathering firewood. My work was with mother setting up our shelter, cooking, and drying the salmon in preparation for winter; but, I loved to watch the men fish at the Falls.*

18

"Many salmon were caught in basket nets, and traps made from fir boughs. These nets and traps were stretched out across the Falls to trap the fish as they leapt against the crashing cascade of water. Salmon that did not leap completely over the Falls fell back into the woven basket nets and traps. Most exciting was watching father and the other men make their way out into the rushing, churning River over slippery, wet rocks.

19

"The men made their way onto narrow platforms made of two
pieces of wood tied together with bark laces. Once there, they
carefully perched over the Falls with spears and gaff hooks.
When a fish was caught, father dropped down on his stomach
for balance, and twisted the barbs of his spear into the salmon's
flesh. In this way father could catch twenty salmon per day.
Another three to four hundred fish were caught in the baskets
and traps.

20

"Fishing in this manner was very dangerous. If a man slipped, he could be sucked into the rushing current below. The strong undertow could easily pull a grown man down, drowning him. If somehow he escaped the pull of the undertow, his body might be smashed against the rocks by the angry waters.

21

"In those days every family in the tribe was rich with salmon.
There was enough salmon caught to last each family until the
next season. Some of the fish was eaten fresh, but much of it was
dried. As a young girl, I helped the women hang the fish on
drying racks. Drying the salmon preserved it through the cold,
snowy winter.

"We celebrated the salmon run, feasting on the fresh-roasted salmon and fresh-water crayfish served up on trays made from the wood of the willow tree. The feast also included huckleberries we girls and women had picked from the hills, and camas roots dug in the valleys and steamed in underground pits. Sacks, woven tightly from cedar and cornhusks, stored the dried salmon for future meals.

23

"The salmon, or In-Tee-Tee-**Huh**, was our money. The fish held great value for us. We traded for hides from the Plains tribes. Later we traded salmon for flour, guns, food, and tobacco from the settlers at the fort.

"Deer and buffalo hides were tanned and made into tepees, saddle blankets, bedding, robes, clothing, moccasins, and ropes. By trading salmon, roots, and berries from our lands for buffalo from the plains, our people had a great variety of foods to last all winter long.

"The Salmon Chief, Kin-Ka-Now-Kla, ruled over the community of people who had come to the Falls to fish and trade. He made sure that the salmon were shared fairly among all of the families.

"Kin-Ka-Now-Kla, our Salmon Chief, was respectful of his people, especially elders, women, and children. The people of the tribe took care of each other. They always shared with those in need.

"*As more and more settlers moved into our lands the fish began to thin out. Each year, fewer salmon were caught at the summer encampments. As I grew older it seemed there were more settlers and less salmon at the Falls each year.*

"*Now, Sinee mat...*" Toopa sighed, and lowered her eyes to the faded picture clutched tightly in her wrinkled brown hands. She stared silently at the photograph for a very long time. "*They tell us the salmon will not come at all.*"

Toopa's words were true. There were no fish ladders in the Dam that was built on our land, across our River. The salmon would no longer come to the Falls to spawn. Our River, our Falls, our salmon, and our homes were to be taken by this Dam. We were promised payment, but it would take the government over fifty years to fulfill this promise.

We moved Toopa up the hill. The water rising behind
the Dam wiped out our village. It flooded the land
where our houses stood at the banks of the River. Our
people could not comprehend this, especially the elders.
When the time came to flood our village, some of my
people had only a few hours to move their belongings
before the new lake took their homes.

Toopa died before my tribe received any payment for what this Dam had taken from us. Today my people live on the shore of an enormous lake created by the largest dam in North America. A few elders remember what life was like when the salmon traveled up the mighty River from the Ocean to the Falls.

When they are gone, there will be no one left to remember this way of life.